Awoke Between The Oak

Between the Oak trees awoke a new world full of mystery and adventure

A story about three girls aged 8-11 who whilst playing at a field at the bottom of their estate discover a magical world which is between two Oak trees and the adventures begin!

By Patricia Newman

Dedicated to my Daughter Clare and her friends who had amazing adventures in the summer.

Contents

Chapter 1

The Discovery

"Come on Jemima, let's go to the river," shouted Molly to her partner in mischief.

"Hang on," replied Jemima in an almost cross voice.

"Are we calling for Lily on the way?" asked Molly.

"No need, she is at the door about to knock," said Jemima.

Jemima is the oldest of the three girls she was eleven years old and is about to begin her first year at Secondary School. Lily is ten years old and beginning her last year of primary school in September. Last, but by no means least, is Molly, she is eight years old, and she was a quiet girl, but also very street wise for a girl of her age. The girls would go to the river, which actually was a small running stream that trickled by the edge of a field not owned by anyone. It was the school holidays and what better way to spend a day, than to call for each other, then wander down to the field or to the river as they called it. At the river they would imagine they were spies and observe people taking their dogs for a walk, unsuspecting, as they walked along in the uncut grass watching their dogs frolic in the sunshine.

It was one certain Sunday that something strange had happened, something that it would be very difficult to explain and at the same time not to be laughed at. Jemima liked to assume the leadership role as she was the eldest.

"Follow me!" she ordered.

Molly and Lily did as they were told and followed a few feet behind. There was a rush of wind as Jemima walked between two very large Oak trees and then silence. Molly and Lily were only few feet behind Jemima, but now she was nowhere to be seen. Lily felt scared, Molly ran on ahead shouting Jemima's name.

"Where are you Jemmy?" Molly shouted very loudly.

There was nothing, all that could be heard was a woman calling her dog Bertie to come back to her. Lily and Molly stood there looking at each other, neither of them daring to speak. Jemima meanwhile was wandering along a street. It was completely different to any street she had ever walked down before. As she looked to her left there was a girl aged around eight selling flowers from a basket. The sky was grey and looked like the clouds were going to burst at any time. The road was cobbled and dirty and did not look clean. Where had she come to? How had she got here? Where was she? These were all questions whizzing around in her mind, all at once.

Jemima carried on walking in a cautious way stepping slowly and observing everything around her. The shop windows were crammed full of different objects to buy. The shop keepers who had no customers were standing at the doors beckoning potential customers in to see their goods.

There was a noise in the distance, she listened intently and after tuning in for a few seconds heard her name being called. Jemima turned around and made her way back down the street she had just walked down and saw the two huge Oak trees she had walked between in the field near the stream before arriving at that this place.

She walked back through the trees towards her friends voices and as if by magic she was back by the two Oak trees.

"Where have you been?" asked Molly.

Lily was also intrigued and asked her, "Why didn't you come when we called you?"

Jemima was so excited and stunned at what had just happened that she was speechless, this did not happen very often! "I walked between the oak trees and I was not in the field any more, but on a street that was very old and dirty. It was full of people wearing old fashioned clothes and the road was all cobbled and hard to walk on."

"Wow! Tell us more," screeched Lily with excitement.

"Why don't you all come back with me and see it for yourselves?" Jemima tempted them. Molly was a little worried, as it was nearly Tea time; she loved her mealtimes and did not want to miss it if she could help it.

Chapter 2

Making Friends

Molly ate her tea with some speed as she was feeling excited at the thought of exploring this strange other place. Lily and Jemima knocked on her front door, they were very excited, but nothing was spoken out loud as they did not want to share the secret.

The three girls walked in a quickened pace, but not too fast as although they were excited they were also a little scared of what this other place might be like. How safe was it? Would they be able to return home if they did not like it? These were questions all of the girls were thinking to themselves.

They stood at the field just in front of the Oak trees each hoping the other one would step forward first. In a short moment of silence the girls grabbed each other's hand and stepped forward in one big step. There was a rush of wind that blew through their hair, but felt warm not scary at all. The next moment they were all stood at the end of the cobbled street looking towards the girl selling flowers, the same girl that Jemima had seen before.

"Hello," Lily said in a confident voice.

"What's your name?" Molly asked.

Jemima did not say a word she just stood there watching all around them.

"My name is Alice," answered the girl in a shy voice. "Would you like to buy some flowers from me?" she asked.

Jemima spoke up and told the girl they did not have any money with them.

"Oh," said Alice, feeling disappointed.

"Why are you selling flowers?" asked Lily.

"I have to, so my mum can buy us food," replied Alice.

Lily was confused with this answer as she did not know any children who had to work. The flowers were very pretty Jemima recognised them as roses. The girl wore a long dress with an apron over the top, probably to keep it clean. The girls all huddled together as they felt a little nervous and sorry for the girl at the same time.

Jemima took charge and said, "come on let's explore."

The three girls walked on down the street, looking in the shop windows, curious about their contents. The road was narrow and quite uneven to walk on. The shop windows were full of interesting items, such as books of all sizes and the covers were catching Lily's eye. Lily really wanted to go inside the book shop, so without saying a word she slowly slipped through the door and immersed herself in the wonderful land of literacy. Lily loved to read and would often let her imagination run wild whilst reading a book. She looked along the fully stocked shelves and was attracted to one book in particular. It was a book about time travel.

Jemima and Molly continued walking along the street, observing every detail, how differently the people were dressed, mostly wearing aprons and beckoning potential customers as they passed by. The girls paused at a shop window dressed with toys made from wood. There was a wooden hoop hanging at the side of the window. The lower shelf in the shop window contained some carved wooden animals, cows, pigs and a horse; they were beautifully made.

Jemima looked round to say something when she noticed that Lily was not with them. Molly was worried and began calling out her name. Lily was so engrossed in looking at the book that she did not hear her name being called. Jemima joined in and shouted Lily's name. Jemima was the loudest and this time Lily looked up and heard her name. She ran out of the book shop clutching the book forgetting that she was in a shop and that the book was not for borrowing, but was for sale. The girls all ran towards each other pursued by the shop keeper. Lily suddenly was very scared and did not know what to do, Jemima on the other hand stayed calm and told Lily to give the book back and apologise for taking it by mistake. The shop keeper was not a cross man, and he accepted Lily's apology. Nothing more was said and the shop keeper walked back to his shop a little out of breath.

Chapter 3

Their Friend Alice

The three girls were having such a strange day with all the new sights to see that they had completely forgotten to keep an eye on the time. Luckily for them the time of the day in this strange but enchanting place was exactly the same as their own home. Jemima glanced at her watch and saw that it was almost half past five so they all decided to make their way back along the street to the tall trees at the end of the road. Holding hands they stepped forward and whoosh they were back in their own time.

The first person to speak was Molly; she asked "can we go back there again?"

Lily answered, "Do you think we should?"

Jemima being the oldest had already decided that they must go back to help their new friend Alice. All three faces were bursting to shout, but they managed to keep it to a smile as they walked to their homes for tea. Luckily, as the only time difference of the other place was that of over one hundred years and not the time of the clock, this meant that the girls could plan their next trip without their parents worrying where they had got to if it was a meal time.

That evening Jemima drew a picture where she lived, there were no cobbled streets and the shops looked so completely different compared to the ones they have visited that day.

Molly had the same idea to draw a picture of where she lived, although her drawing included her family and pets. Lily being the technical one of the group took some photographs of her house and her family with her mobile phone. She thought it would be nice for Alice to see where she lived.

Lily decided to send a text to Jemima saying, "wen r we going bac?"

She loved to used text speak even though it was incorrect spelling, it made her feel grown up as she had seen her older brother use the same text speak. Her mother did not like it at all, but at least Lily could spell the words properly for the times when she was not talking in text. Jemima answered her almost in an instant replying, "soon, 2morrow."

Molly did not have a mobile phone as her parents said she was too young. Molly hoped she would get a phone call to let her know what would be happening next. Lily did phone Molly and asked her if she thought she would be playing out again tomorrow and after a little pause she asked her Dad, she simply answered, "YES."

Chapter 4

Being Prepared

It was nine o'clock in the morning and the girls had met around Lily's house. Lily had suggested they make a picnic for the day so they would not have to worry about getting home for lunch. Lily's mum agreed and made some really nice things. There were cheese and ham sandwiches, crisps of all flavours and some healthy fruit. Molly brought some carrot sticks and cheese spread to dip the carrots in. Jemima loved to eat cheese so she brought some cheese pieces to nibble on.

The food was all packed into their ruck sacks and off they walked to the stream or river as they called it. The sun was shining, not too hot though.

"We're here at last," shouted Jemima.

"It feels like it has been so long since last night when we got back," said Lily;

she was very excited, as usual. They stood there each waiting for the other to step forward and make the first move. Instinctively they all stepped forward in one coordinated step. Whoosh a rush of wind and they had arrived back in time. They had arrived back, and there was Alice holding a large basket of flowers, mostly roses, pink ones and some white ones. "Hello Alice," said Molly.

"How are you?" asked Jemima.

Lily was busy looking for the book shop she had found the last time, the one with the time travel book inside. Alice was really pleased to see her new friends again and asked them if they would like to come to her home to meet her family. All three girls cheered yes at the same time. "I just have to sell a few more roses, and then we will go."

Jemima suggested they go for a walk and meet Alice at eleven o'clock; giving Alice time to sell some more roses, and the girls would have more time to explore a little bit further this time.

Alice did not wear a watch, but there was a clock in the town square so she kept a close eye on the time. She was really looking forward to taking her new friend's home to meet her mother and her little brothers.

Chapter 5

Time For Tea

Molly made an observation that seemed to have gone completely past the other two girls and that was their clothing. It was completely different to the era they were visiting, meaning they would stand out, that was not a good idea at all. She decided to tell Jemima about it as she was the oldest of the group of friends and maybe she would have an idea of what to do about it.

Jemima thought about it for a while and then an idea came to her, they would ask Alice later if she had some clothes to borrow. That morning seemed to go so fast and soon it was time to walk back to the street to meet up with Alice.

Alice had sold most of her flowers, which was a good thing as it meant there would be some money to help pay for some food. When she had invited her new friends back for tea she had forgotten it would mean three extra mouths to feed, but it was too late now.

Lily asked, "how far is your home Alice?"

Alice replied "Not far at all, just around the corner past the bakery."

Lily was so excited to meet Alice's family. Lily was always very excited about new friends and places.

Jemima was about to ask what her brothers names were when they had arrived at Alice's home. It was a small cottage at the edge of the street. The house was very small, but sweet in a homely sort of way. The front door was quite small and Jemima had to bow her head a little in case she bumped it on the low beam.

Alice's mother was in the kitchen decorating a cake as she often did when she had some spare time. Alice said hello to her mother and flung her arms around her for a hug. They would always hug each other each time they left or came back home her mother told the girls. "Hello, my name is Mrs Parker, what are all your names please?" Mrs Parker.

Molly answered first to the surprise of the other two girls. "I'm Molly and I am eight years old."

The other two girls then introduced themselves. Alice's brothers came running into the kitchen as they had smelt the delicious smell of the freshly baked sponge cake.

Alice shouted out "STOP!" to the boys as she was worried her new friends would be knocked over in the rush. The brothers were three and five years old, full of life and energy as boys are at their age.

"Mother, when we can have some cake?" asked Thomas the youngest.

Edward added, "my tummy is so hungry!"

"Soon", answered their mother, "very soon." "Alice would you like to show your friends your bedroom?"

"Yes alright, follow me." Alice took the girls to her bedroom; it was right at the top of the house in the roof.

"This is amazing and so beautiful Alice," said Jemima.

Lily was really quiet for a change she was not herself at all. The covers on Alice's bed were white cotton and embroidered around the edges, beautiful thought Lily.

Jemima asked Alice if she had any clothes they might borrow as the ones they were wearing were a little bit conspicuous. Alice had already decided to lend all of the girls some clothes as she didn't want her friends to be noticed too much when they went back into the street, as she had seen some of the people in the streets staring as they had walked to her home.

"Lunch is ready!" shouted Mrs Parker,

"We are coming down in just a moment mother." Alice answered.

The girls had all chosen something to borrow and were quickly changing. Mrs Parker had made beef stew for Lunch. The girls really enjoyed it. The pudding was the best though a delicious homemade Victoria sponge cake with jam in the middle and sugar sprinkled on the top.

Lily was a big fan of food, but especially homemade cakes, her mum didn't make many cakes even though she always would ask her for some. Edward and Thomas ate so quickly that their tummies did not feel full at all and wanted more, but their mother said that this had to last for tea tomorrow evening as well. At this point Jemima noticed how sad Mrs Parker looked. Alice noticed to, "are you alright Mother," she asked.

"Yes I am fine thank-you Alice; you are always so concerned for me." said Mrs Parker confidently.

Alice did not ask her again that evening as she knew what the problem was. After tea the girls went back up to Alice's bedroom, Molly asked her why her mother was a little sad at tea time. Alice explained that her father had died a year ago and her mother had to look after the family all by herself. The house they lived in was rented from a landlord who was not very nice at all. His name was Mr Bridges. He would collect the rent each week and tomorrow was the next time he would be knocking at the door for the money. The past week Alice had sold as many flowers as she could, so there was just enough to pay the rent.

Lily decided it was a good time to show her some photos of her family she had taken on her mobile phone the day before. Alice was speechless; she had never seen anything like a mobile phone before. It was then that the girls realised that mobile phones had not been invented yet. Lily clicked through the photographs on her handset. It was nice for Alice to see Lily's family, even if it was on a strange contraption.

Molly showed Alice her drawings she had done and said she could keep them as a present. Jemima took out her drawing of where she lived. Alice was fascinated by the streets, how different they looked, with no cobbles on the road to make you twist your ankle if you were not concentrating as you walked! Alice really enjoyed talking to her new friends and loved exciting things they were telling her.

The time had flown by and it was almost six o'clock in the evening. They went downstairs and thanked Mrs Parker for a delicious tea and hoped that they would see her again soon.

"Is it alright if I walk my new friends some of the way home?" asked Alice.

"Of course it is, you silly thing," said Mrs Parker.

"I won't be long mother," Alice called out. The girls followed by and all said thank-you to Mrs Parker in unison. They were a little worried as they should have been home by now. Alice stopped in the main square and watched as her new friends disappear around the corner and into the clump of trees.

They all waved and shouted, "see you soon Alice."

There were the oak trees and whoosh the wind blew in their ears and they were back, home from another day of adventure.

Chapter 6

Cakes

"Isn't Mrs Parker the most amazing cook?" Jemima said to Lily as they walked to call for Molly.

It was nine o'clock in the morning and Molly was not the best at getting up early. As Jemima and Lily knocked on the door.

Molly answered it in her pjs and dressing gown. "Why are you here so early?"

"Well we had an idea," whispered Jemima.

"Molly, would you like to come out to play with us?" asked Lily.

"I will just ask Mum," answered Molly.

"Mum, can I go out with Jemima and Lily today please?" Molly shouted in a wishful tone .

"Only when you have some clothes on darling," replied her mum.

Molly let her friends into the house to wait for her whilst she had a quick wash and got dressed. It only seemed to take a few minutes for Molly to present herself as ready to go out. They all said bye to Molly's mum and off they walked along the road to the bottom of the estate to where the special oak trees were. Whilst walking along the road Jemima began to think about the horrid man called a landlord who Mrs Parker had to pay money to so they could live in their home. She then began to think aloud and asked the others if they had an idea of how they could help Mrs Parker, so that she did not have to worry about paying the rent for the house. Lily suggested that as Mrs Parker was such a good cook, why she could not sell her cakes in a shop.

"What an excellent idea Lily." Jemima said in a positive voice.

Molly suddenly stopped walking. They had arrived at the field where the Oak trees stood. "What's the matter Molly?" asked Jemima.

"I don't know," answered Molly.

She had a scary feeling that went all over her body; she could not explain it at all. Jemima sometimes forgot how much younger Molly was than them and she realised now that Molly had become frightened at the thought of the horrid man called a landlord.

"Aren't you coming along Molly?" asked Lily.

"Don't worry about Mr Bridges he only visits Mrs Parker to collect money to pay for the house," Jemima said, trying to reassure Molly.

"Alright, let's go, at least we get to see Alice our new friend," replied Molly now excited.

The girls approached the Oak trees cautiously, but with commitment for their decision to visit their friend Alice and her family. They all held hands and stepped forward, whoosh the sound of the wind rushing around them and they had arrived.

"Race you to Alice's house," shouted Jemima to the other girls.

Molly forgot about her fear and ran as fast as she could after Jemima. Lily was such a chilled out girl and decided to just gently jog behind her friends, she was in no hurry to be out of breath from running if she did not have to. Jemima knocked on the door as they arrived at Alice's house.

Mrs Parker opened the door and greeted the girls with a smile. Molly spoke first and asked if Alice was at home.

"No" replied Mrs Parker, "she is in the main square selling some cakes I had made earlier."

"Oh", exclaimed Lily.

"We didn't see her on the way here and we had just come through the main square." said Jemima.

"Why don't you girls take these buns I have just baked for her to sell and maybe you would all like to come back for something to eat." suggested Mrs Parker.

"Alright that's what we will do," decided Jemima and the other girls both agreed.

Lily volunteered to carry the tin of buns for Alice to sell and off they walked back to the main square. Mrs Parker listened to the girl's idea of selling buns and cakes in the market square from their last visit and Alice was having no trouble in convincing buyers to buy her mother's cakes.

It was about an hour later that Alice had sold all of her mother's cakes and it was nearly lunchtime. The girls walked back with Alice to her home and when they got there they saw that a man was standing at the door. He was wearing a tall black hat and a long brown smart coat; he also seemed to be leaning on a walking stick. His face was mostly covered with a neatly trimmed beard, that made his face look very unearthly. He was aged about Sixty and his grey hair could be seen peeping out from the edge of his hat. His long coat hid his rounded body; apart from it looked like it would not have fastened.

Alice whispered, "that is Mr Bridges."

Molly suddenly felt very worried, as she had remembered what Alice had said the last time they visited. Jemima put her arm around Molly and Lily just stood there observing him taking in every detail of what he looked like, how he spoke and also what he said.

"Mrs Parker." he said in a quiet, but commanding voice. "Have you got the rent?"

Mrs Parker looked at Alice and went towards the tin in the sideboard cupboard; she took off the lid and counted out some notes.

"Here you are Mr Bridges," she said as she nervously handed over the rent money.

Mr Bridges thanked her in a quiet voice.

"Oh, and one more thing, I have decided to increase your rent by double the amount and I shall be back next Friday for the next payment." Exclaimed Mr Bridges, he said goodbye and turned around and walked away.

There was a huge sigh of relief from everyone who stood in the room, the smile that Mrs Parker had greeted the girls with had disappeared and was replaced a sad look.

Alice tried to cheer her mother up but telling her about the cakes she had sold. "Mother, I have sold all of the buns and cakes today."

Mrs Parker's face changed in an instant to a smile, Alice handed over the money. It was more money than Mrs Parker could have ever imagined just for baking some cakes. Reassured by this Mrs Parker asked Alice to set the table and they would have something to eat. Lily's mother had packed a picnic lunch, enough for everyone to share. Lily un-wrapped some sandwiches with ham and cheese as fillings and also some apples from her garden. Mrs Parker was very grateful as she was wondering how she would have enough to feed everyone. The money from the tin was all she had left for the rest of the week to feed her family and pay the rent. Thankfully now Alice had sold all of the cakes she was beginning to believe that some of their troubles were nearly over. Thomas and Edward really seemed to enjoy the picnic Lily had brought with her.

"Are you going to bake some more cakes for me to sell tomorrow mother?" Alice asked.

"Yes of course," replied her mother, "we need every penny we can earn from the cakes to pay for this house; in fact I am going to begin baking right away." Mrs Parker had a new look on her face, one that Alice had not seen for a very long time. It was an expression of happiness and satisfaction.

After lunch the girls all went upstairs to Alice's bedroom and they dressed up in some more of Alice's clothes. Molly had remembered to bring back the clothes she had borrowed from Alice the day before. Lily and Jemima said that would bring the clothes they had borrowed back the next time they came to visit.

The time seemed to go so fast when they were visiting Alice and her family and soon it was approaching four o'clock and so they said their goodbyes and walked back towards the market square. Jemima had an idea she decided to speak to one of the market traders to find out how Mrs Parker could get a place to put a table for selling her cakes. The woman she spoke to told her she would have to talk to the Town Hall Clerk; and they would let her know what the cost was of having a stall in the market, but also if there was a space to be rented.

Jemima was excited about hopefully being able to help her friend Alice and her family to be earning enough money to not have to worry about paying her rent and maybe even being able to buy her house. Lily noticed how close they were to the edge of the town and where the trees were. She held out her hand to Molly and Jemima and they all stepped forward together into the void and back home to their time.

Chapter 7

The Market Stall

Jemima was in her bedroom when she had a thought, what was a Town Clerk?

"Mum!" shouted Jemima, "What is a Town Clerk?"

Jemima's mum looked puzzled at such a question.

"Why do you ask?" she answered.

"Well someone said it the other day." Jemima shouted back.

"Well a Town Clerk is a person who works in the Town Hall and decides who can do various jobs, for example if they can work on a market stall." Jemima's mum said effortlessly. Jemima's eyes lit up as if there had been a torch behind them. She could not help herself but smile at her mothers's answer.

"Thanks mum, is it ok if I call for Molly and Lily?" Jemima replied.

"Of course you can," answered her mother.

Jemima ran to Molly's house and knocked on the front door. Molly's mum answered the door.

"Can Molly come out?" asked Jemima.

Molly's mum called upstairs to Molly as she was in her bedroom drawing pictures of their adventures. Little did Molly's parents know that they were real adventures!

"Hold on I am just finishing my colouring." answered Molly.

"Ok I will call for Lily and see if she can come out to so we can all spend the day together. Back soon." said Jemima.

Jemima ran round to Lily's house and there was no need to knock on the door as she was in the front garden planting some flower bulbs.

"Do you want to come and play Lily?" asked Jemima.

"Maybe later. I just want to finish planting these bulbs," answered Lily.

"See you later Lily, bye." replied Jemima, she was disappointed in her friends not wanting to come out, but she understood as they had spent the last week together going out every day.

Jemima wandered by herself to the field where the trees were and just sat watching the people walking with their dogs, throwing sticks and waiting for the dogs to run after them. She watched as a woman threw a giant stick for a tiny dog and how the dog dragged it back to its owner. Jemima laughed and as it happened out loud because the owner of the little dog gave her a stern look until she saw the funny side of watching the tiny dog us all its strength to drag the stick along the ground and deposit it in front the woman.

Jemima wondered what would happen if she went to the place on her own. She was at an age when she seemed to be curious about lots of things. She had a quick look around to check there was no one around, then she took one step forward and she could hear the wind increasing around her and the familiar whoosh they heard every time they had walked between the trees swirled all around her.

She felt scared this time as she was on her own, but she knew she had a job to do and that was to find the Town Clerk and speak to him about getting a market stall for selling cakes.

Jemima took a deep breath and said to herself out loud, "I can do this!"

At this point she had not noticed the elderly man watching her talking to herself. He grinned and thought to himself, "I am glad I am not the only one who talks to myself."

Suddenly, Jemima stood in front of a very large dark brown door. On it was a name plate saying, 'Town Hall'. She was there and began to feel a little bit nervous and wishing her friends had been stood beside her. She always felt there was safety in numbers. Her hand reached up to a large door knocker in the shape of a ribbon, one end on a hinge so the knocker could move. Jemima stood on her tip toes and grabbed the knocker and pulled it back towards to her, it sounded very loud when she let it go and it fell against the door.

A man dressed in a black suit answered the door. "Can I help you miss?"

Jemima hesitated as she could feel her knees wobbling as she stood there. "Erm, could I talk to the Town Clerk please?"

"No you have to make an appointment," answered the man at the door in a flat tone of voice. "Oh," replied Jemima, "Can I make an appointment please?"

"What is your business?" asked the man curiously wondering why a young girl wanted to speak to the Town Clerk.

"Cakes!" answered Jemima simply.

"Come back at Three o'clock today," answered the man.

The door slammed shut and Jemima stood there in amazement at how brave she had been.

She gazed at her watch and the time was only Eleven in the morning so she decided to make her way back home to her time and see if her friends were ready for some more adventure.

Jemima was walking at a steady pace, when suddenly she saw the landlord, Mr Bridges.

He noticed Jemima and said in a quiet, but stern voice. "I hope Mrs Parker has got the rent money for me when I collect it next Friday."

Jemima remembered she was not to talk to strangers, and particularly this one who she felt frightened of. She broke into a trot toward the trees and did not look back. Moments later she arrived at the field, panting as if out of breath, but it was fear of Mr Bridges and not the exercise.

Chapter 8

The Appointment

The sun was shining, but it kept hiding behind a large cloud allowing the rays to peep through the edge of the cloud. It made Jemima stop and think about what she had to do that afternoon before time ran out.

The Man at the Town Hall had said she must go back at Three o'clock, but she did not want to go back on her own. It was lunch time so she went home to have a sandwich before calling for her friends. Her mum was out at work, but her dad was home and he was in the middle of making a ham and cheese sandwiches. Jemima thought to herself what good timing in getting home when she did, as she was feeling quite hungry, she ate her sandwich as quick as a flash and she was shouting to her dad, "I am calling for Lily and Molly, bye see you later."

"Tea is at Six tonight Jemmy." replied back her dad.

Seconds later Jemima was knocking on Lily's front door. Lily answered it and asked her mum if she could go out for the afternoon with Jemima.

Lily's Mum hesitated, but after a pause she said, "Yes, but be home for tea at half past Five." Lily agreed and out the door she ran.

"We have to call for Molly," said Lily as they ran down the street, but before either of the girls had knocked Molly opened her front door and stood there waiting for their next words. "Can Molly come out to play?" asked Lily.

"Mum; can I go out with Lily and Jemima?" Molly asked feeling hopeful.

Molly's mother answered, "Yes but you must be home for Five o'clock."

Molly grabbed her purple jacket and off they all jogged down the street until they reached the field.

The girls all held hands and stepped forward between the Oak trees and waited for the whoosh. Nothing happened!

"Why is it not working?" asked Molly.

Maybe it was because there was a man walking his dog close by.

"Maybe it's because we are not alone as we usually are." replied Jemima.

Thinking of the appointment Jemima picked up a stick and threw it as hard as she could and hoped the dog would see it and chase after it. Luckily the dog did exactly as she predicted and it ran as fast as it could to catch the stick. Its owner saw what Jemima had done and began to chase after his dog as it was going out of sight. The girls held each other's hands and stepped forward and whoosh they heard the sound of the wind as they were pushed back through time once again to where their friend Alice and her family lived.

All three of the girls sighed with relief at arriving back at the place back in time. Jemima had told Lily and Molly about the visit to the Town Hall and arranging the appointment for three o'clock for Mrs Parker to ask about how to rent a market stall to sell her cakes. As they walked through the market square they saw Alice selling cakes from two baskets.

"Hello Alice," Lily said. "We are off to see your mother about a market stall."

"How many more cakes have you got to sell?" asked Jemima.

"Only three." replied Alice.

"Good as it is Half past two and we need to go to your house." said Jemima.

Alice was curious about this statement, but didn't say anything. Mrs Parker was in her kitchen mixing the next batch of cakes to sell.

Jemima spoke first. "Hello Mrs Parker. You have an appointment at the Town Hall at Three o'clock."

"What are you talking about Jemima?" asked Mrs Parker.

"I was at the Town Hall earlier, and I asked about how to get a market stall selling your lovely cakes and the man I spoke to said you have to have an appointment with the Town Clerk to discuss it." Jemima Replied.

The time was almost quarter to three and the girls really wanted Mrs Parker to go to the appointment.

"Please go to the appointment Mother." pleaded Alice.

Mrs Parker gave in and said "Alright, alright, I shall go to the appointment, but I wish someone had asked me first."

Mrs Parker put down the mixing spoon and put on her hat and coat. The girls walked at a steady pace trying to encourage Mrs Parker to do the same. Thankfully the Town Hall was not too far away from where Mrs Parker and her family lived. The time was five minutes to Three o'clock, as they arrived at the door of the Town Hall. Jemima knocked as Mrs Parker felt nervous.

"I have an appointment with the Town Clerk at Three o'clock this afternoon." said Mrs Parker in a quiet and shaky voice.

The man who answered the door replied in a loud booming voice. "Ah yes it was arranged this morning by your daughter, follow me, this way."

At the Town Clerk's office door, the man knocked and a voice said, "Come in." Mrs Parker asked the girls to wait outside whilst she went in as it would look better for her case. The girls sat on a wooden bench outside the Town Clerk's office. The time seemed to drag on for ages. In fact Mrs Parker had only been in the office for a matter of minutes discussing how much it would cost for her to have a market stall in the Town square.

The door suddenly opened and all of the girls jumped out of their skins. Mrs Parker said good-bye. The Town Clerk and had the biggest smile Alice had seen for a very long time. "Come along girls, let us go home and celebrate." Said Mrs Parker as she had found out that she could rent market stall for only Two Pounds a month.

They arrived at Mrs Parker's home and still smiling Mrs Parker got out a cake that looked so special, too good to eat, but Mrs Parker was determined to cut a piece for everyone to have some. At that point Alice's brother came in from playing outside.

"Thomas and Edward wash your hands! We are having a piece of cake to celebrate," Mrs Parker said.

"What does celebrate mean?" asked Edward.

"It means we are going to have a market stall to sell mother's cakes on," replied Alice. Everyone looked down at their plates as a piece of cake was placed onto them. Jemima suddenly looked at her watch and saw that it was Four o'clock already. Molly has to be home for Five o'clock for her tea she thought to herself. Mrs Parker was already planning her stock for the stall as she would be taking it over on the Friday of that week. Lily asked Jemima what the time was as she had remembered she had to be home at half past five.

"It is time we said good-bye for now as our parents are expecting us home for tea very soon." Jemima said.

"Well you must not be late home," said Mrs Parker.

The girls ate every last piece of cake on their plates, said goodbye to everyone and walked towards the square and stopped just in front of the Oak trees. They held hands and stepped forward, 'whoosh' the wind surrounded them, and the next minute they were stood in the field at the bottom of their estate.

Chapter 9

The Order

It was nearly time to go back to school after the long summer holidays. It had been an adventurous time this year with the discovery of the time portal for the three friends, but they did not want to go back to school without knowing that Alice and her family would be alright and not under the pressure that Mr Bridges the landlord put Mrs Parker under.

It was the Thursday of the last week before returning to school, Jemima and Lily were at Molly's house doing some colouring pictures to take back to Alice on their next visit.

"When shall we go and see Alice?" asked Molly

"How about later when we have finished our pictures." said Lily.

"Excellent idea, I have nearly finished mine," answered Molly.

It was another half an hour before all three girls had produced beautiful pictures. Molly went downstairs and asked her mum if she could go out with Lily and Jemima.

"Tea is at six o'clock so please don't be late as I am cooking something special, your favourite, bangers and mash." her mum replied.

"Thanks mum, see you later!" said Molly

The girls left and ran to Jemima's and Lily's parents to check they were all alright to go out as well. All was well and each child had permission for their afternoon out.

The sun was still shining, but it was not as warm as it had been during the earlier summer months, so the girls each took a light jacket with them, just in case. Walking to the field made each of the girls feel a little nervous, giving them a feeling of butterflies in their tummies. Nervous because they wondered whether the special time travelling portal would work and how their friend Alice would be.

They had arrived, it was time to walk between the Oak trees and visit their friend Alice and her family for what they were beginning to feel was getting closer to an ending as the new chapter of a school term was about to begin.

The three girls held each other's hands and stepped forward so they were directly between the trees. They always felt a little worried, but also excited to be seeing Alice again.

Whoosh went the wind as it blew in their faces whisking them back in time. This time was the first time Molly took notice of what the tunnel looked like as she had always closed her eyes before on previous times. She could see the bright colours in various shapes along the side of the moving tunnel in which they travelled back in time. The colours were all the shades she had ever seen, making strange shapes like spirals which had no endings. It made Molly feel a little bit dizzy so she decided to close her eyes as she usually had done.

In the time Molly had been thinking and watching the sides of the tunnel they had arrived at the time where Alice and her family lived. Lily had been thinking what it would be like to bring Alice back to the future and if it would even be possible. Jemima also deep in thought was wondering how the market stall had been going, and whether Mrs Parker had been selling lots of her delicious homemade cakes.

None of the girls had realised when they arrived on the other side of the time travel tunnel that there was a huge queue of people and lots of excitement about which cake to buy and whether there would be enough left once they reached the front of the queue. Whilst moving forward to the front of the queue, without pushing in they could see it was Mrs Parker's cake stall. Mrs Parker was very busy serving customers, but caught a glimpse of the three girls as they stepped forward. She smiled at the girls and whispered a thank-you to them all. Jemima smiled back and asked if she would like some help on the stall.

"Yes please girls that would be lovely, I will take the money and you three could help by placing the cakes in the wrapping paper to keep them fresh for customers to carry the home safely." replied Mrs Parker.

Lily was happy to see her friend Alice, but as they were all busy helping they would save their conversations for later.

There seemed to be a never ending queue of customers until the last sponge cake was sold, over two hours later. Mrs Parker began to put all of the empty cake tins together with the help of the girls. Her sons meanwhile were playing with a hoop; chasing it around the market square with great delight, especially when either of them caught it. Just as the last tin was put into a large carrying bag in a basket a tall figure darkened the empty stall.

He spoke in a deep voice. "Excuse me madam, but is this your stall?"

"Yes it is Sir," Mrs Parker replied.

"I would like to order some cakes for a function that is planned at the Town Hall this Saturday." the man said.

"Of course Sir how many, and what type of cakes would you like to order?" Mrs Parker asked.

The tall man answered in a clear tone of voice. "I would like to order Twenty large sponge cakes and thirty small bun type cakes."

Mrs Parker wrote down the order and asked the man his name and at what time he would like them to be delivered to the Town Hall on Saturday.

He then said "The function is at two o'clock in the afternoon so will you deliver them at twelve o'clock, my name is Mr Copley."

"Certainly Mr Copley, would you be able to leave a small amount of money towards the order?" asked Mrs Parker.

"Here is two pounds; the rest will be paid on Saturday with the delivery." he added.

"Thank-you Mr Copley, if you do not mind waiting for a moment I will prepare a bill for you." Mrs Parker quickly worked out how much the bill would be for Mr Copley and handed it to him.

Mr Copley smiled as he said thank-you and walked back towards the Town Hall. Mrs Parker could not believe her good luck and began singing to the girls as they helped to gather the rest of the bags and baskets. Alice had not seen her mother so happy for a very long time. "Alice, as you just heard we have a large order of cakes to bake for Saturday as well as run the market stall tomorrow, would you mind helping me to bake some cakes for tomorrow?" Mrs Parker Asked.

"Of course Mother, can my friends help as well?" asked Alice.

"Oh yes, can we, please?" asked Lily, she loved to bake cakes.

"That would be lovely thank-you girls, thank-you very much for everything; I could not have done this without your help," added Mrs Parker.

Jemima spoke up first and said. "It was your delicious cakes that did it, we only gave you the idea and maybe a little nudge along the way."

Mrs Parker looked a little puzzled at Jemima's comment of a nudge, but she thought it must be a nice word and smiled whilst opening her arms for a group hug. The market stall was packed away and the girls helped each other to carry the bags and baskets to Alice's home. Thomas and Edward followed on behind still chasing their hoop as it rolled along the road.

Molly looked at her watch and the time was Three o'clock, all of the girls had to be back home by at least half past five so as it was still early they rolled up their sleeves and began to weigh out the ingredients for the next batch of cakes.

Mrs Parker wrote down the ingredients and each of the girls took it in turns to weigh each item out. It was like a production line in a factory, everyone working together in a team. None of the girls argued, each just got on with their given task and the cake baking began. The kitchen had a most delicious smell and the girls were beginning to feel hungry. At this point there were four large sponge cakes in the oven and Mrs Parker, who was also beginning to feel hungry, decided it was time for a quick snack and something to drink for everyone.

Mrs Parker boiled a kettle and made a cup of tea for herself and poured out some fresh milk for the girls and boys to drink with a couple of slices of bread and butter each.

Jemima checked her watch and it was almost Five o'clock, she told the other girls to eat and drink up their snack as they had to go home for their tea.

"Goodness is that the time already, you must make your way home as you do not want to be late or your parents will be worried also thank-you for your help today, many hands make light work," Mrs Parker said as the girls finished their snack.

"Thank-you for our snack Mrs Parker, it was lovely, just what we all needed to keep us going until we get home." Molly said in a loud and happy voice.

The girls checked they had their jackets and each hugged Mrs Parker in turn as they said their goodbyes until they came back again. The girls found themselves running back towards the market square as the time seemed to be racing along. They did not want to be late for tea, but they so enjoyed their visits to Mrs Parker and her family, especially their friend Alice.

They stepped forward holding each other's hands and closed their eyes, Molly had no hesitation in closing her eyes this time after the dizziness she had felt on the beginning of her journey. They arrived back at the field. It was raining and slightly colder than this morning, but they didn't mind as their day had been full of excitement and happiness.

Chapter 10

The End Is In Sight

It was Saturday, the day of the function at the Town Hall.

Jemima sent a text to Lily saying, "r u ready 2 go?"

Lily answered straight away, "I am on my way round to u now."

Lily remembered that Molly did not have a mobile so she called for her on route; thankfully they were all ready to go at the same time. Lily recalled that Mrs Parker had to deliver the cakes to the Town Hall at Twelve o'clock so as it was Ten o'clock; they knew they would have enough time to help carry all of the lovely cakes.

The girls walked at a brisk pace and stopped as they reached the Oak trees, without saying a word to each other they reached out their hands and held tightly before stepping forward between the trees. They all decided to keep their eyes closed after the dizziness Molly had told them about when she had opened her eyes in the time tunnel. Whoosh, they all felt and heard the wind as it filled the air around them.

The sun was shining as they arrived and the girls moved from a fast walk into a trot as they got closer to Alice's home. Molly knocked on the front door.

Alice shouted, "I will get the door mother." As Alice opened the door she could see it was her friends Molly, Lily and Jemima standing there. "Mother, the girls are here."

"Come in, come in girls, I am glad you are here as I really need your help. I have packed the baskets, but I still need some extra help to carry them to the Town Hall." Exclaimed Mrs Parker.

The girls were more than happy to help Mrs Parker and Alice, even Thomas and Edward planned to carry a basket each.

There were all sorts of cakes; large jam sponge cakes, small fairy cakes that had been iced with a sugar glaze, bread style buns with cream and jam in the centre; in fact the cakes all looked so delicious that the girls' tummies were rumbling, but they knew these cakes were special and they must not eat any of them. What they did not know was that Mrs Parker had made some extra cakes and before setting off to the Town Hall, Mrs Parker offered the children a glass of milk and a cake of their choice from a different tin. Thomas and Edward went first as they had the hungriest tummies, noticed by their constant asking for something to eat.

"Thank-you," each child said in turn as they chose their cake to eat.

"This is to keep us filled up until we come home for luncheon." Mrs Parker said.

The children all drank up their milk and Mrs Parker finished her cup of tea and the loading up of the cakes began. Luckily it was not a long way to the Town Hall only a Ten minute walk, made slightly longer by carrying the baskets.

Mrs Parker went up to the side door that she had been told to use for the delivery of the cakes by Mr Copley. She knocked loudly and they all waited for an answer. Mr

Copley came to the door and recognised Mrs Parker immediately.

"Mrs Parker, Thank-you for being so prompt today, this is a very important function and I have been looking forward to sampling your cakes after the words I have heard about how good they are. You can bring the cakes in here and place them out on the table at end of the main hall." Mr Copley said, Mrs Parker smiled at Mr Copley and ushered the girls and boys in to where they needed to unpack.

Whilst the girls were unpacking the delicious looking cakes Mr Copley approached Mrs Parker with smile.

"Mrs Parker, here is the rest of the money as we agreed on Thursday in the market place." said Mr Copley excited to eat the cake.

"Thank-you Mr Copley, I hope you and your guests enjoy them." Mrs Parker replied.

The cakes were displayed beautifully on the table each labelled to what they were. Just as Mrs Parker and the children were gathering up the baskets.

Mr Bridges appeared. "Mrs Parker!" a loud voice boomed in the main hall.

"Hello Mr Bridges." replied Mrs Parker. Inside she was trembling with fright.

"What are you and your brood doing here?" said Mr Bridges in an angry tone.

"I am delivering cakes for the function here today." said Mrs Parker still shaking with fear.

"Pray tell, who ordered cakes from you?" asked Mr Bridges in a stern voice.

"Mr Copley ordered the cakes on Thursday." answered Mrs Parker confidently.

"COPLEY!" screamed Mr Bridges.

"Yes Sir." answered Mr Copley in a quiet voice.

"Who told you to order cakes from this woman?" shouted Mr Bridges.

"Erm no-one, I had heard talk of how good the cakes were and decided that they would be perfect for today's function." answered Mr Copley.

"I see!" said Mr Bridges as he looked sternly at Mr Copley who was also a little frightened of Mr Bridges.

Before Mr Bridges could say another word, the Mayor who had overheard the loud voice of Mr Bridges, approached them and asked "Is there a problem?"

"No sir, a problem?" said Mr Bridges in a sudden worried voice.

"Yes I heard the way you were speaking to Mrs Parker and may I say I am not happy with the tone of your voice," the Mayor spoke in a calm way.

The children were stood quietly waiting for Mrs Parker to say it was time to go. The Mayor greeted all of the children pleasantly as he was a kind gentleman and was not impressed at Mr Bridges and his manner of speaking. Mrs Parker felt relieved that the Mayor had come over to speak to Mr Bridges; he also was a regular customer of hers every day as his wife would buy a box of assorted cakes for their tea in the official office at the Town hall.

"Mrs Parker how are you?" asked the Mayor. "I am so very pleased that Mr Copley ordered the cakes for this function from you."

Mr Bridges began to visibly shrink even though he was wearing a tall hat.

"Mr Bridges please could you apologise to Mrs Parker for your raised tone of voice," the Mayor said in a quiet, but commanding voice.

"Mrs Parker, I would like to apologise for my tone of voice as it was unkind and

unacceptable." said Mr Bridges apologetically.

"I accept your apology Mr Bridges, however I am unsure of the next day you will be collecting the rent." asked Mrs Parker.

"Excuse me Mrs Parker, did you say rent?" asked the Mayor.

"Yes I did Sir." replied Mrs Parker.

"How much do you pay for your cottage Mrs Parker?" asked the Mayor.

"I presently have to pay £2 each week." Mrs Parker said confidently.

The Mayor had a look of confusion on his face. "I am sorry Mrs Parker my hearing is not very good at the moment. Did you just say £2?"

"Yes Sir," answered Mrs Parker.

"Who collects this rental money from you each week?" asked the Mayor.

"Mr Bridges collects this money." said Mrs Parker and what she had not realised was that the Mayor owned the house which they were renting and not Mr Bridges.

"Mr Bridges, I would like a word with you please?" said the town Mayor sounding unhappy.

"Please excuse me Mrs Parker, I shall return in a few moments." The Town Mayor said in a calm tone.

The Mayor and Mr Bridges walked over to one of the offices in the corridor, the door closed behind them. The Mayor's voice could be heard asking Mr Bridges who had told him to ask for so much rent money.

Mr Bridges could only squeak the answer "no one Sir." The Mayor was extremely cross with Mr Bridges, so cross that he asked him to leave his employment immediately and to never return as he did not follow the rules of the job of only collecting the rent thats asked of, not to collect more money to buy yourself luxury foods to make yourself at a higher standard than the average towns folk.

Mrs Parker waited patiently for the Mayor to return. She saw Mr Bridges leaving the building looking sad.

The Mayor walked over to Mrs Parker and apologised for the dealings she had endured with Mr Bridges. "Thank-you Mrs Parker for your honesty in the case of Mr Bridges, I have a proposal to make, I believe you have been living in the cottage for some time and I would like to make you an offer of becoming the owner of the cottage for the money is already paid in the rental. What is your decision?"

Mrs Parker wobbled with the shock of what the Mayor had just said.

"Mrs Parker are you alright?" asked the Mayor. "Please Mr Copley would you fetch Mrs Parker a chair to allow her to steady herself."

Mrs Parker sat down and as she sat she realised exactly what the Mayor had just said to her.

"Sir did you just say I could become the owner of the house instead of paying rent money?" Mrs Parker said delighted.

"Yes I did Mrs Parker," said the Mayor.

"Yes Sir, thank-you very much." Mrs Parker said with the biggest smile ever.

He continued speaking by saying he would draw up some deeds to the house and have them delivered first thing Monday morning to be signed. The Mayor held out his hand to Mrs Parker and shook her hand as a bond of what he had just offered.

The children all seemed to jump into the air at the very same time, cheering "HOORAY." Then they all gathered the baskets up as they had fallen over in the excitement of what had just happened

"Mother, does this mean we do not have to pay rent anymore?" asked Alice.

"Yes it does, the Mayor has given us the house to be our own." replied Mrs Parker with tears in her eyes.

Another loud "HOORAY!" could be heard and the children could not stop smiling all the way back home.

Mrs Parker opened the front door and put down her empty cake basket and turned to the three girls Jemima, Molly and Lily. "Ever since you have been visiting us we have had good luck and good fortune, I must thank-you for everything."

Jemima answered first and said, "It was your delicious cakes which have done this, not us."

"Thank-you Jemima, but it is you and you friends who have given me the confidence to do more than I would ever have dreamed. We will see you again soon won't we?" asked Mrs Parker.

Lily replied, "I do hope so we really enjoy our visits to you and your family especially Alice." Everyone began to hug and say good-bye for now until the next time.

The three friends waved as they left Alice and walked slowly back to the edge of town. It seemed only a couple of minutes that they had left Alice, and they were now standing back in front of the Oak trees. They stepped forward holding hands and closed their eyes. Whoosh went the wind as it rushed around them and they arrived back on the field in their own time. "Let's go home for tea and get our stuff ready for school on Monday." said Lily.

Even though the summer holidays had been full of adventure she was really looking forward to going back to school on Monday. The friends said goodbye as they parted to go home, each happy knowing they had helped a family and made some new friends for life. When would their next adventure happen and where would it take them.

The End

Printed in Great Britain
by Amazon

42560816R00040